P9-DWW-545

CALGARY PUBLIC LIBRARY

APR — - 2014

CUENTO DE LUZ

To Alba Sellarés, beloved and sadly missed librarian,
who loaned out books and gave away smiles.

- Mar Pavón -

To my friend Xamón, who witnessed this tale.

- Alex Pelayo -

I Want to Be Philberta

Text © Mar Pavón
Illustrations © Alex Pelayo
This edition © 2013 Cuento de Luz SL
Calle Claveles 10 | Urb Monteclaro | Pozuelo de Alarcón | 28223 | Madrid | Spain
www.cuentodeluz.com
Original title in Spanish: Ser Filiberta
English translation by Jon Brokenbrow

ISBN: 978-84-15619-73-4
Printed by Shanghai Chenxi Printing Co., Ltd. March 2013, print number 1352-2

All rights reserved

FSC
www.fsc.org
MIX
Paper from
responsible sources
FSC® C007923

I Want To Be Philberta

MAR PAVÓN & ALEX PELAYO

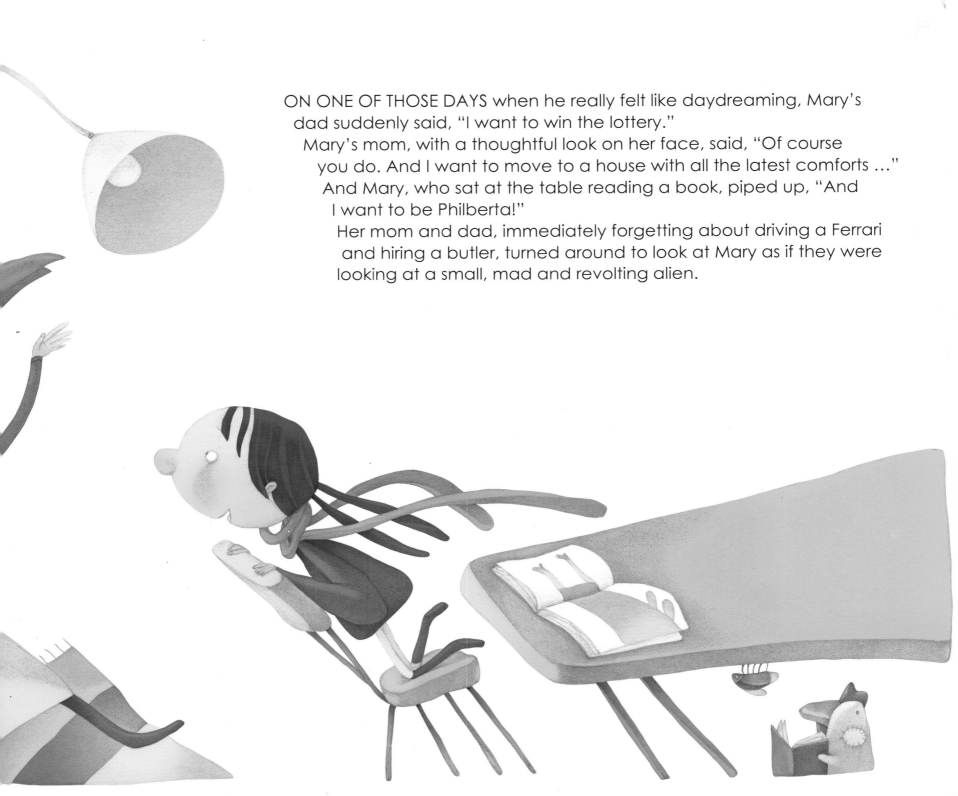

ON ONE OF THOSE DAYS when he really felt like daydreaming, Mary's dad suddenly said, "I want to win the lottery."
Mary's mom, with a thoughtful look on her face, said, "Of course you do. And I want to move to a house with all the latest comforts …"
And Mary, who sat at the table reading a book, piped up, "And I want to be Philberta!"
Her mom and dad, immediately forgetting about driving a Ferrari and hiring a butler, turned around to look at Mary as if they were looking at a small, mad and revolting alien.

Later that morning at school, the principal said to Mary's teacher, "I swear I just want to retire once and for all." The teacher quickly replied, "Oh really? Well then, I want to be the new principal!"

Mary, who was passing by with a book under her arm, couldn't help herself and blurted out, "And I want to be Philberta!" The principal and her teacher, both forgetting for a moment about retirements and promotions, glared at Mary as if she were the strangest creature that had ever crawled upon the face of the earth.

That afternoon in the park, two old men were chatting on a bench.
Suddenly, in a fit of sincerity, one of them turned to the other
and cried, "I want to be young again!"
The other old man answered back, "Aha! And I want my dearly departed
wife to come back to life!"
Mary, who happened to be sitting on the grass in front of the bench, reading
a book to a tiny kitten, yelled with all her might, "And I want to be Philberta!"
Forgetting their dreams about falling in love again and the delicious food their
wives had cooked, the old men looked at the little girl as if she had a screw loose.
Why would she say something like that? And even more peculiar, who would ever
think of reading a story to a kitten?

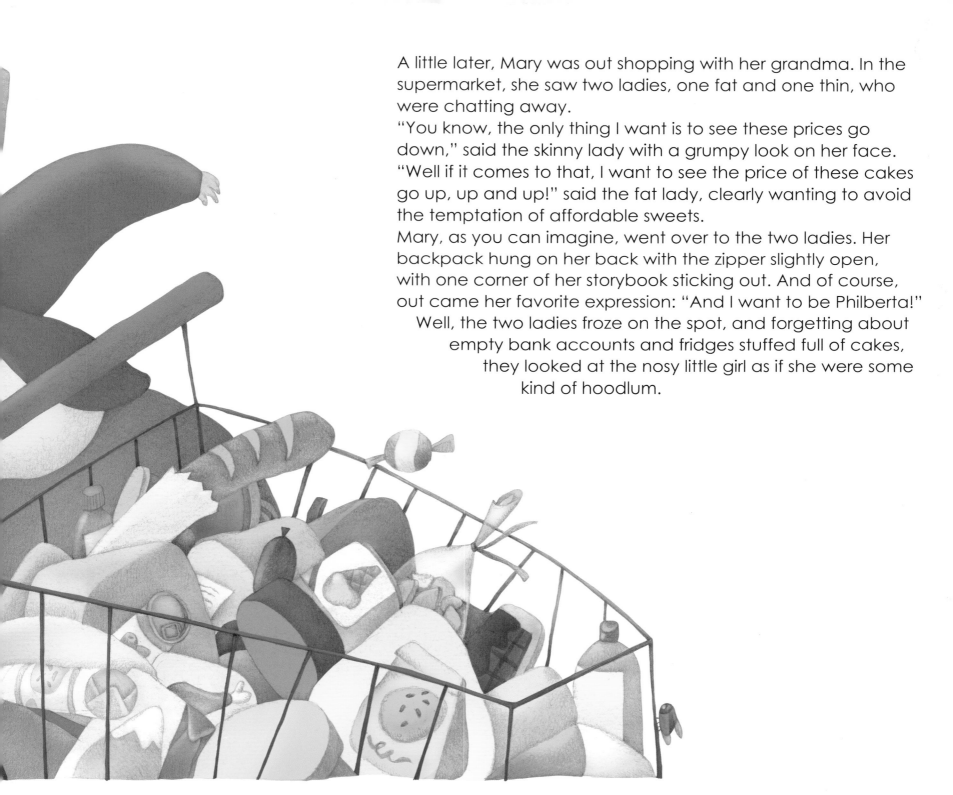

A little later, Mary was out shopping with her grandma. In the supermarket, she saw two ladies, one fat and one thin, who were chatting away.

"You know, the only thing I want is to see these prices go down," said the skinny lady with a grumpy look on her face.

"Well if it comes to that, I want to see the price of these cakes go up, up and up!" said the fat lady, clearly wanting to avoid the temptation of affordable sweets.

Mary, as you can imagine, went over to the two ladies. Her backpack hung on her back with the zipper slightly open, with one corner of her storybook sticking out. And of course, out came her favorite expression: "And I want to be Philberta!"

Well, the two ladies froze on the spot, and forgetting about empty bank accounts and fridges stuffed full of cakes, they looked at the nosy little girl as if she were some kind of hoodlum.

That evening at Mary's grandparents' house, a neighbor knocked on the door and yelled at Mary's grandma, "I want you to give me back the tablecloth I lent you a century ago!"

Mary's grandma, without blinking, answered back, "And I want you to give me back the teapot I lent you *two* centuries ago!"

Mary's grandpa, who'd heard everything from the living room, jumped up and joined in with the same angry tone, saying, "And I want to watch the TV in peace, so you two can take your tablecloth and your teapot and go make a cup of tea where I won't hear from you in *three* centuries!"

Mary, who'd seen the whole affair while clutching a storybook to her chest, jumped between her grandparents and their neighbor and shrieked with all the strength she could muster at six years of age, "And I want to be Philberta! Philllberrrtaaaa! PHILLLBERRRTAAAAAAAA!!!

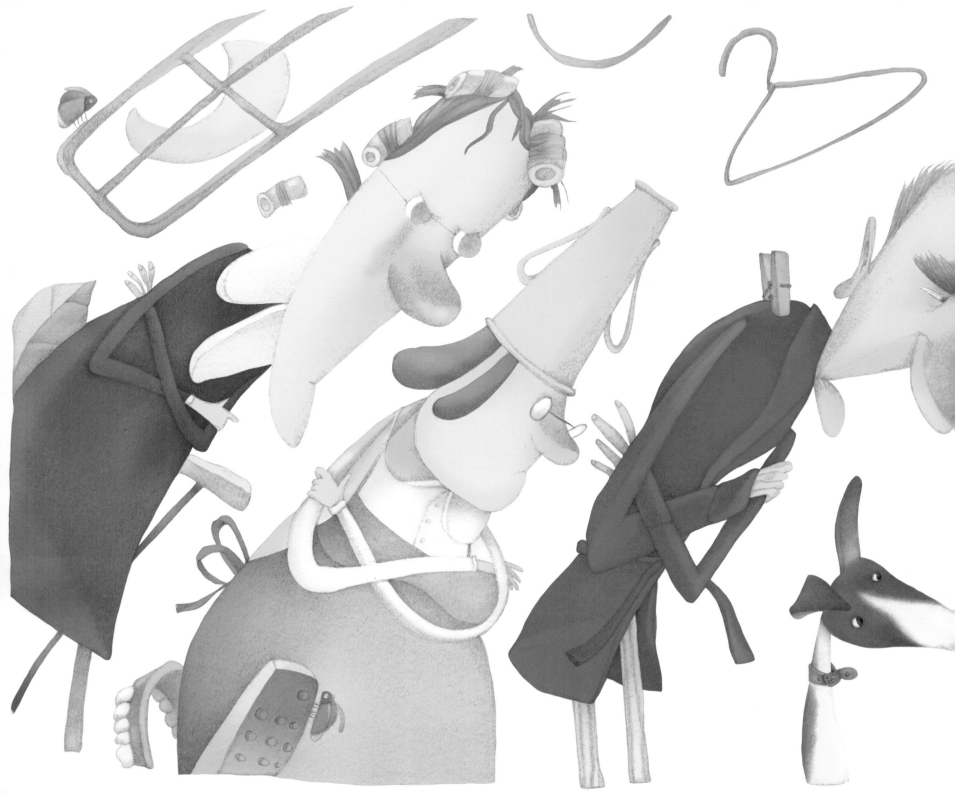

Well, as you can imagine, the neighbor forgot all about her tablecloth, her grandma forgot all about her teapot, and her grandpa forgot all about his favorite TV show (that one for gentlefolk of a certain age called "High Flying Grandparents," which he'd never seen all the way through since he always nodded off during the first commercial break). What really mattered was that they saw how their sweet little Mary had suddenly changed, for no apparent reason whatsoever, into a rude, noisy little witch — the terrible witch Philberta, without a shadow of a doubt!

That night, Mary's mom and dad were at their wits' end; they'd seen their little girl behaving most strangely, they'd received an urgent note from her school, signed by her teacher and the principal himself, they'd received a huge telling off from one skinny lady and one fat lady, and they'd received a worried message from her grandparents and their neighbor — all in the same day!

"I want to take Mary to a personality disorder specialist!" her dad said anxiously.

"And I want to take her to an expert in behavior problems!" groaned her mom.

"AND I WANT TO BE PHILBERTAAAAAAA!!!" yelled Mary from her bed, where she'd swapped her favorite toy, a woolly sheep for ... a storybook, of course!

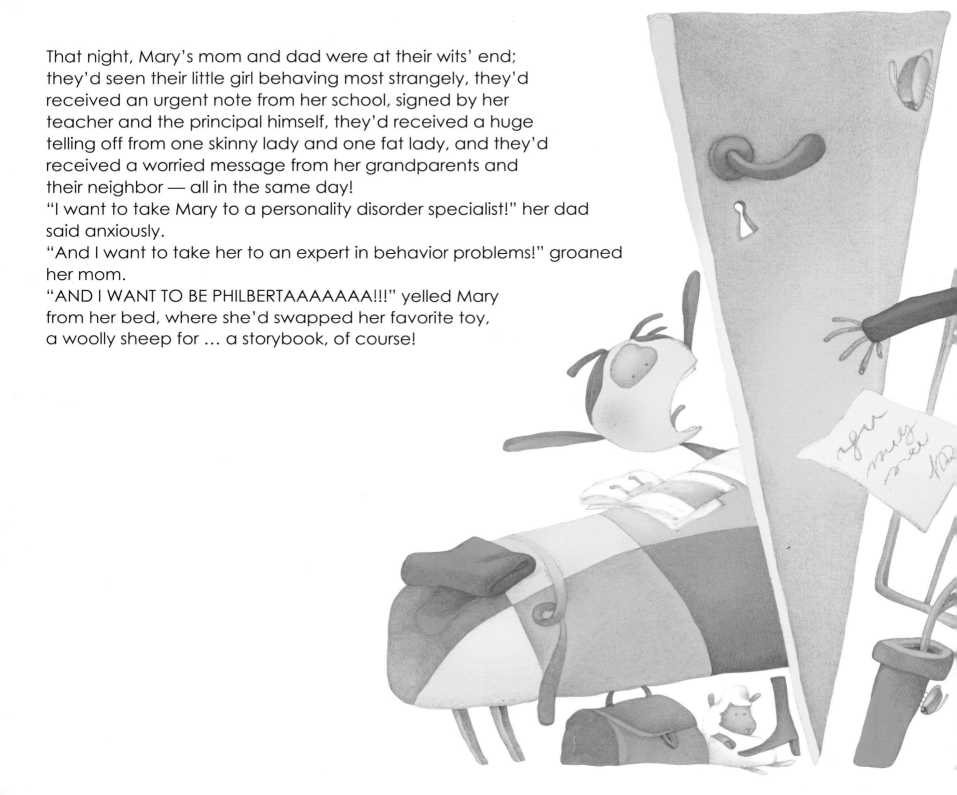

The following morning, Mary found herself sitting in front of two very serious looking men wearing white coats: a disorder-curing doctor and a problem-solving doctor, according to what her parents had told her. They sat in the waiting room, and they weren't alone. They were with her teacher and principal, the two old men from the park, the ladies from the supermarket, her grandparents, and of course, their neighbor. And all of them were itching to know what on earth was up with Mary, and how it all would end.

"I'd like to know what's wrong with you, young lady," said the disorder-curing doctor in a kind voice.

"And me too, of course. That's what they pay me for!" said the problem-solving doctor, trying to sound funny.

"And I want to be Philbertu," said Mary in a very grown-up voice, putting a storybook down on top of the table.

"And why do you want to be Philberta, instead of Philomena, for example?" asked the disorder-curing doctor.

"Or instead of being from the Philippines?" said the problem-solving doctor, once again trying to sound funny.

Mary answered them immediately: "Because people make lots of impossible wishes and Philberta grants wishes to all of the people around her!"

"Oh really? And what does Philberta look like?"

"Yes! What's she like? Is she *philugly*, *philpretty*, *philtall*, *philshort*, *philblonde* or *philbrunette*?"

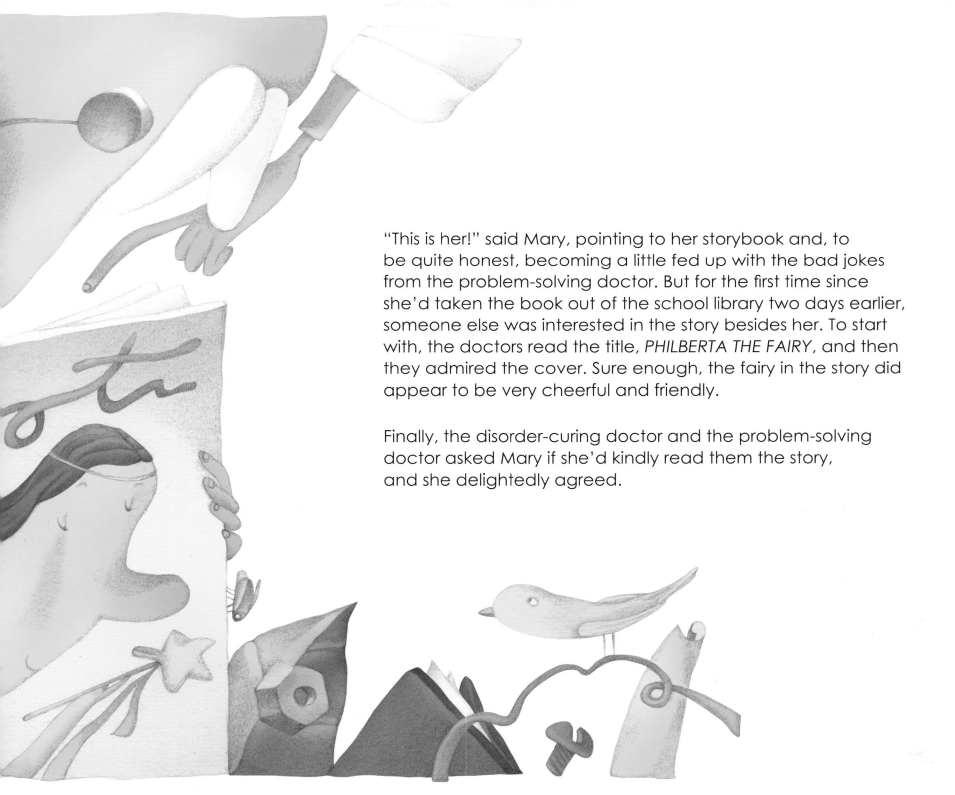

"This is her!" said Mary, pointing to her storybook and, to be quite honest, becoming a little fed up with the bad jokes from the problem-solving doctor. But for the first time since she'd taken the book out of the school library two days earlier, someone else was interested in the story besides her. To start with, the doctors read the title, *PHILBERTA THE FAIRY*, and then they admired the cover. Sure enough, the fairy in the story did appear to be very cheerful and friendly.

Finally, the disorder-curing doctor and the problem-solving doctor asked Mary if she'd kindly read them the story, and she delightedly agreed.

Meanwhile, in the waiting room, nobody could understand why the doctors were taking so long to come out and announce their diagnosis. As we know, everyone had their own theory: Mary's mom and dad thought that she was actually an alien, her teacher and principal thought she was some kind of weird creature …

… the two old men were sure she wasn't right in the head, the two ladies from the supermarket assumed she was an out-and-out hoodlum, and her grandparents and their neighbor still suspected that Mary was secretly studying to become a wicked witch!

By now, someone else had joined the group that was waiting for Mary. A few minutes earlier, a mother and father had arrived with their young son, who was carrying a storybook under his arm.

The crowd of people waiting for Mary began to get impatient, and nervously started saying to each other: "We want to know what's up with Mary!" Then they began to grumble more loudly: "We want to know what's up with Mary!" Soon, waving their fists in the air, they began to shout:
"WE WANT TO KNOW WHAT'S UP WITH MARY!"

"AND I WANT TO BE WIIIIISEBURRRGEEEEEEEERRR!!"
Immediately, the room fell silent. Then everyone turned around to see who
had yelled so loudly. There, standing in front of them, was the little boy
who had just arrived, with a storybook still under his arm. Or was he
some kind of monster, carrying a book of evil deeds waiting
to be done? There was no way of telling anymore!

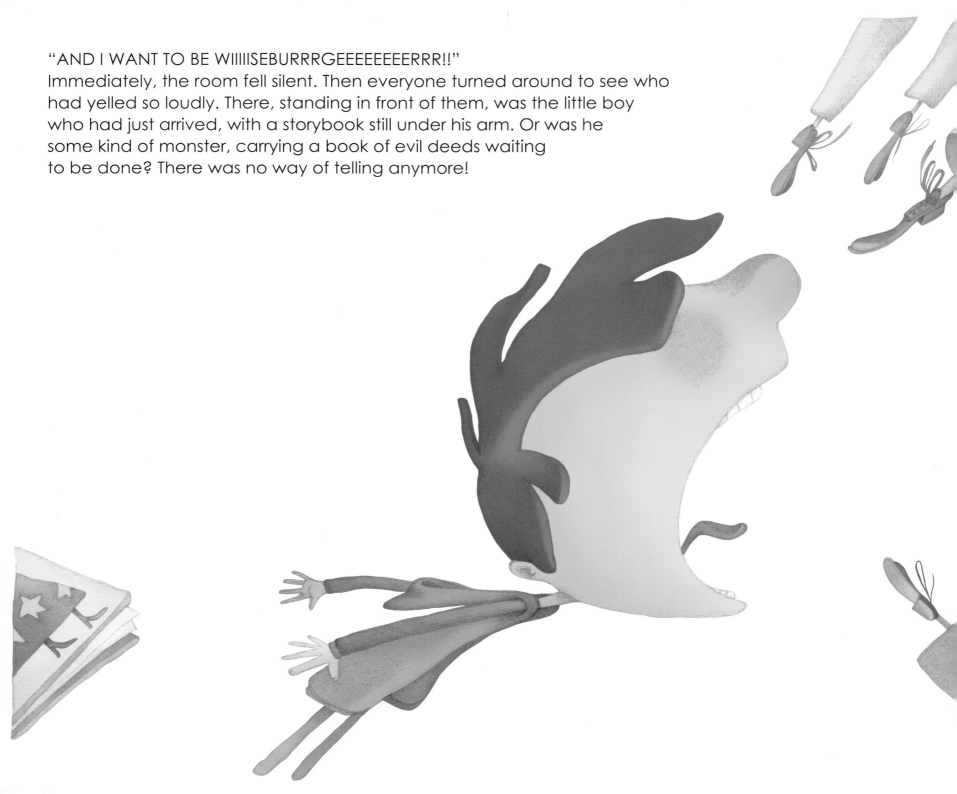

But then, just as the little boy's red-faced parents were about to apologize for his outburst, the doctors' office door opened, and out stepped the disorder-curing doctor and the problem-solving doctor, followed by Mary with her storybook in her hands. Funnily enough, now everyone was absolutely quiet, as the crowd outside the door still had not recovered from the shock of the little boy yelling about wanting to be someone called Wiseburger! "We – we'd like to know what's up with Mary," stammered her mother after a long, nervous pause.

"Nothing's up! Mary just wants to be Philberta!" replied the disorder-curing doctor as if it were the most natural thing in the world.

"And we can't do anything except … let her read her story and become Philberta, at least for a little while!" added the resident smarty-pants, the problem-solving doctor.

And in the blink of an eye, they flung Mary into the air and she stretched out her hands to show everyone her beloved book.

"This is the story about Philberta the Fairy," she announced happily.

"AAAAAAH!!!" exclaimed the crowd.

"And this is the tale of Wiseburger the Wise!" piped up the little boy, grinning from ear to ear and showing off his book as his parents lifted him into the air.

"OOOOOOH!!!"

But the best part of all was when someone began to chant:

"READ THEM OUT LOUD! READ THEM OUT LOUD!"

Boy, did they read those books! And boy, did everyone enjoy them! And at least on that unforgettable morning, the disorder-curing doctor and the problem-solving doctor didn't have to cure anyone or solve anything. And another thing: Mary and the little boy became the greatest of friends. So much so, in fact, that they often swapped their favorite stories with each other.

And from that day on, whenever the grown-ups in this story woke up with funny ideas going around in their heads, they went straight to the nearest library or bookshop and came home with a book. Reading made the time fly by ... and seemed a much better way of passing the time they'd previously dedicated to making silly wishes that would never come true!

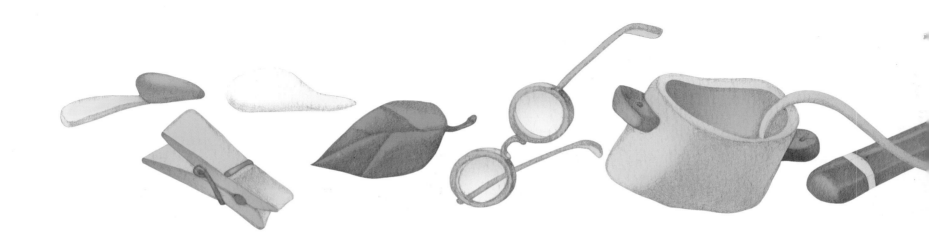